THE BRUMBACK LIBRARY
OF VAN WERT COUNTY
VAN WERT, OHIO

THE PARKERSTOWN DELEGATE

THE PARKERSTOWN DELEGATE

BY

GRACE LIVINGSTON HILL

A Christian Endeavor Story

Amereon House

F
H/L

Originally Published Boston, 1892
Copyright 1981 by Amereon Ltd.

Library of Congress Catalog Card Number 81-70360
International Standard Book Number 0-89190-064-0

AMEREON HOUSE,
the publishing division of
AMEREON LTD.
Box 1200
Mattituck, New York   11952

Designed and Manufactured in the United States
of America by The Mad Printers

*Dedicated to all of the ardent fans
of Grace Livingston Hill who have
kept alive her memory and spirit.*

THE PARKERSTOWN DELEGATE

CHAPTER I

The shadows are long and low on the grass, the sleepy road is muddy, the chestnuts look expectantly down from the laden tree with their eager, prickly faces, all ready to leap when the frost shall give the word, the river glides dreamily along, and the rusty throated crickets sing and sing the whole day. A busy gray spider works hard to finish certain meshes on the railing of the upper porch. Nothing makes any difference to her anyway. She builds her house in a convenient place for catching flies, and when that house fails or breaks she builds another, so on to the end, and then it is all over.

Two men came down the road in blue jeans overalls and checked blouses. One is big, with a large neck and no collar, a sunburned face lengthening into sandy whiskers, a broad coarse straw hat and hands in his pockets. The other is younger, with a pleasant face, a manly figure and a spade over his shoulder. They both have large, heavy boots spattered with mud, and walk much with their heels, carrying their feet after them with a sort of a rhythmic curve, shaped something like a tie in music.

"Is Lois coming back soon?" asks the younger of the two men as they near the large white house on the right hand side of the road. There is much hesitation in his manner as he asks the question, but he tries to summon a matter-of-fact tone, and swings his body a little more decidedly.

The large man, however, does not notice, for he suddenly seems aroused to a piece of news he has forgotten to impart.

"Well, yes, now you mention it, she is." There is a pleased look in his pale blue eyes and a broad grin of satisfaction over his face as he makes this reply. He is very proud of his daughter Lois, and three months is a long time for her to have been away from home. He wishes all the neighbors to understand that it is a great thing for Lois Peters to be at home once more. "She's coming on this evening's express train, and that's what I'm hurrying home so early for."

There is a glad ring in the young man's voice which he cannot repress as he answers: "Well, I declare! I'm right glad of it. You see Harley's been taking on so of late because she's been gone so long. He says it seems as if she would never come any more."

"You don't say!" says the proud father.

"Well, now, that's too bad. I'm glad she's coming. I make no doubt she'll run right over and see him the first thing. How is the little chap these days?"

"Pretty poorly. He doesn't get any better. Some days he's able to be dressed and move about, but most of the time he has to be quite still. Mother gets discouraged about him, but the little fellow is as patient as can be. Father says he can't bear to look at him, sometimes, it seems so dreadful to think he can never be well again."

"Yes, it is pretty hard," said the rough

man, rubbing his checked sleeve across his eyes; "uncommon hard for the little chap. Well, good evening! Lois will be right glad to see you over, I have no doubt. She'll come right off to see the little chap, too," and the two men parted, the younger at his father's gate, while the older man passed on down the road toward the village.

"So Lois is coming back again. Well, I'm glad of it," said the young man to himself as he paused a moment by the gate and looked meditatively back up the road he had just come. The distant hills were purpling themselves into their nightcaps, while the sun tore the clouds into scarlet and gold ribbons to adorn them. The young man watched the process a moment as he had watched it many times before, but to-night the gold seemed more glorious than it had for many a sunset eve, and perhaps it was because it reminded him of the light on Lois's face. At least his heart felt that the sunlight of the village was coming back. He had not thought much of it in that way before, it is true; but he was glad, nevertheless, perhaps for his little brother's sake, that Lois was coming back. They had been good friends for years.

There was nothing handsome about Franklin Winters except his great, honest dark eyes, and his smile. People said his smile was like a benediction. That smile lighted up his whole

face as he turned to go into the house, and
made him look handsome. Although he was
not a well-educated young man, and although
when he talked he did not always use the best
of English, still the slow, even tone in which
he spoke his words and the rare smile with
which they were often accompanied, took the
sharp edge from what would otherwise have
grated on the refined ear, and made one feel
that here was true heart culture at least, if
there was not overmuch education.

It was pleasant, too, to see the tender-
ness with which he approached the bed of his
young invalid brother, after he had removed
the great straw hat which covered his well-
shaped head, and stood some minutes at the
kitchen sink, making a half-way toilet before
the cracked looking-glass.

"Harley, I've some good news for you,"
he said. "Lois is coming home tonight on the
evening express, and her father says he's sure
she'll run right over here the first thing. Maybe she'll come in the morning."

The joy of the young invalid was quite
apparent. He had very few pleasures in his
monotonous life. Ever since the scarlet fever
had attacked him, several years ago, his had
been but a weary, painful existence.

He was not much more than thirteen years old, but his life of pain had made him old in many ways beyond his years, while the constant necessary reliance upon others had kept him quite a child too. He had the same dark, handsome eyes as his brother, but his face, though a trifle thin and pinched with the pain he had suffered was beautiful as any girl's.

"O, Frank, I'm so glad!" he exclaimed, catching his brother's hand and squeezing it. "Now she'll have more stories to tell, and maybe some new plans for me. I'm so tired of all the old ones, and besides I've outgrown them. Three months is a long time when one has to spend it on the bed, you know, and can use the nights to live in as well as the days — that is, most of them" — and he smiled a sorry little smile.

"On the evening express did you say she was coming?" he asked again suddenly as if a new idea had struck him. "Then why couldn't you carry me into the other room for just a little while and let me watch it go by? It would be such fun to see it and then to think that there was someone I knew in the lighted-up cars. I've watched it before, you know, but I didn't ever have any one in them to feel that way about. Why it would be 'most as good as going in a train myself, as I did when I was such a little fellow before I was hurt, with father. I can remember real well about how the cars looked, and if I could see the express go by tonight and could think she was in it, maybe I could imagine myself in those cars whirling along beside her, coming home from the city like any boy. Say, Franklin, you will, won't you? It won't hurt me to be moved tonight, a bit, for I've had a real good day," he finished triumphantly, and then looked up to his brother's face with such pleading in his eyes as could not be resisted, albeit the brother's were so full of tears that he was forced to turn his head the other way for a moment.

"If mother says so, Harley," he managed to get out, and then strode from the room to find the mother and choke down his rising feelings.

Harley had his wish, although the troubled mother doubted the wisdom of it when she saw the fever into which her boy worked himself before the train did finally rush by. And then it was such a passing pleasure, with all the imaginings of himself on board. A few sparks, a few shrieks, a roar, a rush, a bright quick glancing of lighted windows with dim figures in them, and then all was over, and Harley could scarcely get to sleep, so excited was he.

He was awake very early the next morning. He knew the colors of the sunrise well, and could tell you all about them, for he had watched them many times from his window, after long nights of weary hours, which it had seemed to him would never end. He watched the pink bars of the sky slowly turn to gold, and then melt away into a glory that burst over the world and filled everything, even his room, and brightened his pale face for a little. Then the world waked and went to work and things began. Harley might hope for Lois to come soon, for had she not been his friend for so long, and did she not love him dearly? And Lois did not disappoint him. She came while it was still early, with a great spray of chestnut burs in her hand, that the frost had opened and robbed of their nuts just to show the world what a pretty velvet lining was inside.

Lois had not exactly a beautiful face when you considered it carefully; her skin was pink, and her eyes blue, with yellow lashes, and her hands just the least mite freckled, like her father's, but the eyes were bright and sweet, and the lashes had somehow caught and tangled a sunbeam into them, and the hands were quick and graceful, nevertheless; besides Lois had hair — wonderful hair! It began by being red like her father's, but the glory of the sunlight was in it to mellow it, and the soft brown richness of her mother's had turned it down, until the red only shone through in little glints, and made it the most beautiful halo of soft, rippling light about her head; so that when you considered her hair, Lois was lovely. Harley thought her very beautiful, and I am not sure but his brother Franklin held the same opinion.

"And now, Lois," said Harley, when the greetings were over, and they had settled down to an old-time talk, "begin! What will you tell me first? Let me see. Begin with the nicest thing first. What was the nicest thing you saw in all the time you were gone?

Lois raised her eyes a little above their level, and put on her thoughtful expression. Harley liked to see her so, and feasted his eyes upon her as she studied the ceiling, thinking how good it was to have her back with him again.

But Lois's eyes were beginning to brighten and a smile crept over her face which Harley knew was the harbinger of some good thought or story.

I think the convention was the best of all," she said, bringing her eyes back to his face, full of pleasant memories for him to read.

"Convention! What convention?" asked

Harley almost impatiently, "and how could a convention be the pleasantest thing in a visit to a big town?"

"But it was," said Lois emphatically, "the very best thing of all. I think if I had to choose the whole of the rest of my visit and those three days of convention I wouldn't have stopped a moment to think, I would have chosen the convention — at least, that's the way I'd do, now I've been to it."

Harley looked puzzled. He could not understand why a convention should be particularly interesting to a girl, but he had unlimited faith in Lois and her taste.

"Was it politics, or a firemen's convention? And did they — why, I suppose they had a great many parades, didn't they? Was that why it was so nice?" he asked, trying to understand.

"O, no, indeed!" said Lois, laughing. "It wasn't politics nor firemen nor Farmers' Alliance nor any of those things. It's a long story, and I'll have to begin at the beginning. It was the State convention of the Y.P.S.C.E. Do you know what those letters mean?" and she stopped to watch the color deepen in Harley's cheek and his eyes shine as he tried to guess what the mystic letters could mean, but after he had made several unsuccessful attempts she went on.

"It means Young People's Society of Christian Endeavor," she said naming each word on a finger of her hand, and nodding triumphantly as she finished. "Do you know about it?"

"No," said Harley. "It sounds stupid. I can't see how you could like it so much," and there was almost a quiver of disappointment about his mouth.

But Lois hastened to take up her story and make its scenes live again before the eager eyes of her small listener.

CHAPTER II

"It's a very big society," she began; "there's one all over everywhere pretty near. They even have one in Japan, they say. It's a society of the young folks all working for Christ. That's what Endeavor means, you see. It's a long story, so if you don't understand all I say you better ask questions, for I may leave out some. All the young folks get together first and say, 'We'll have a society,' and then they take the pledge and the constitution and" —

"What's the pledge and constitution?" interrupted Harley.

"I don't know much about the constitution," said Lois, "I guess it's just their laws; but the pledge I've learned by heart:

" 'Trusting in the Lord Jesus Christ for strength, I promise Him that I will strive to do whatever He would like to have me do; that I will pray to Him and read the Bible every day and that, just so far as I know how, throughout my whole life, I will endeavor to lead a Christian Life.'

"That's the first half. I didn't learn the rest. It's about being at all the meetings and helping them along, and always going to the consecration meeting once a month, unless you have an excuse you can give to God. I didn't think it was worth while to learn that part, because we haven't any society here and I don't suppose we ever shall have. They don't take to such things in this town, but I thought the first half of that pledge anybody could take and be a society by one's self, so I have written it down and signed my name to it, and I'm trying to be a Young People's Society of Christian Endeavor all by myself. Well, about once in so often — once a year, I guess it is — they have a convention. There's a great big one of all the societies in the country, in some big city — that's what they call the 'National' — but this wasn't one of them. This was a state convention. That means just the societies in that State, you know. Mrs. Brant said she invited me to come to town early in the season so that I could be there to the convention, because she thought I would enjoy it; and I did, ever so much. Well, the first meeting was in the evening, and they began to come — the delegates — along in the afternoon from the trains that came in from all directions. Maybe you'd see a young man with a satchel, and then three girls, and then two or three youngish boys, and you'd run to the window and say, 'There come some delegates! I wonder if they're the ones that'll come here to our house!' You see Mrs. Brant kept three of them, two young men, and a girl that

roomed with me, and I got pretty well ac-
quainted with her and she told me all about
their society at home and" —

"But what's a delegate?" interrupted Harley again.

"Oh! they're the folks each society sends
to represent them. The whole society couldn't
come, of course, because it would cost too
much and they couldn't all be entertained,
and then some of them would have to stay
at home any way, I suppose; so each society
sends two or three of its members, and they
call them delegates. Some of the delegates
were very nice. They all wore badges just like
the Grand Army men when they go to a big
meeting, only those had Y.P.S.C.E. on them
in big letters and the name of the town they
came from, and some of them had a motto.
It was ever so nice to study their badges and
say to them, 'You live in Newtown, don't you?
Why, I have a cousin there. Did you ever see
her?' I heard from two people I used to know,
that way. It was real exciting that first night
before I got used to it. Mrs. Brant had raised
biscuits and doughnuts and thin slices of ham
and some of her nicest preserves for supper,
and there was the best table-cloth and the
biggest napkins, and the whole house looked
so 'receptiony.' The three delegates looked as
if they enjoyed it, too, when they came down-

stairs with their hair all combed, and their eyes shining as if they'd just got to the front hall of Heaven and expected to be shown a good way inside before the next three days were over. We had to hurry through supper, for the first bell began to ring early, and it kind of made us all uneasy to get there and begin, we'd heard so much about it and talked it over so long. I'd meant to take real solid enjoyment eating one of those doughnuts, for Mrs. Brant does make such lovely ones, but I was so in a hurry to get to meeting that I actually didn't finish mine.

"The first thing that night was a sermon, and it was a good one. I do wish we would have such preaching here in Parkerstown. It just made me feel as if I wasn't any kind of a Christian, though I have been a member of the church for four years. Why, all those young folks are doing so much and living so differently from what I am, that I felt all sort of left out. I haven't remembered much of the sermon itself — not the words — but that's the way it made me feel, and I never shall get away from the feeling that came that night that I mustn't waste any more time living the way I'd been doing.

"When we got home, after we'd had a talk awhile in the parlor with the delegates, and they'd gone to bed, we got breakfast as near ready as we could the night before, so we could go to the meeting at six o'clock in the morning. When I heard about that meeting I thought it was a dreadfully silly idea to begin so early, and I made up my mind that whatever else I went to I wouldn't go to that meeting. I thought I'd have enough without it, but Mrs. Brant said she wanted me to go; that they said it was one of the best meetings of the whole thing, and I felt a little curious about it after the delegates began to talk so much of it, and so we decided to go, and slip out ahead to have breakfast all ready for them when they came back. And we did. You ask about parades. They weren't exactly any parades, only when church was out they looked a little that way, everybody with badges, you know, but before those morning meetings there was just a procession of folks going. It was interesting to see them. I stood in the door and watched while the last bell was ringing, and the people came hurrying from all directions. There was a family opposite that Mrs. Brant says never go to church, and it was funny to see them come to the door, and the man poked his head out of the upper window to see if there was a fire or anything that people were all out so early and the bells were ringing. They found out after a few hours, though, that the bell would keep on ringing all day.

"It was the most beautiful meeting that I had ever been to, then. The leader read the twenty-third psalm, about 'The Lord is my shepherd,' you know, and then we sang, 'I was a wandering sheep,' and the leader asked them all to pray, and they did, ever so many of them. I think there were twenty or thirty prayers right in a minute or two, and they didn't try to pray long and ask for everything in the world at once, but each one had some little thing he wanted for himself, or for them all, that he asked for. Then they sang, 'There were ninety and nine,' and the leader told them that as there was but half an hour for the meeting anyway, that they must all be quick and short, or everybody wouldn't have a chance, and they all were.

"A girl spoke up just as he got through, and said she had been thinking while he read the verses, how she had heard that it was the lambs that kept close to the shepherd that he cared for most tenderly. He found nice things for them to eat, and he took them up and carried them when they were worn out, and when there was danger they always felt safe, and she thought it was a good deal so with following Jesus; the ones that kept close to him had an easier time and loved him better than those that only followed far away. Then one of our young men delegates recited a beautiful poem, and it was so pretty I asked him to write it out for me. I can only remember a few lines of it, but you shall have it all to read when I unpack my trunk. It began like this:

" 'I was wandering and weary
    When my Saviour came unto me
For the ways of sin grew weary
    And the world had ceased to woo me:
And I thought I heard him say,
As he came along his way,
    O silly souls! come near me;
    My sheep should never fear me;
    I am the shepherd true.

" 'He took me on his shoulder,
    And tenderly he kissed me;
He bade my love be bolder,
    And said how he had missed me;
And I'm sure I heard him say,
As he came along his way,
    O silly souls come near me;
    My sheep shall never fear me;
    I am the shepherd true.'

"There was an old man who sat way back, and he said, right after that, that he didn't want to take up the time of the young folks as he knew he was an old man, but he had been a shepherd himself once, and he

knew all about sheep. He said they wouldn't
ever lie down until they had had enough to
eat and were quite comfortable, and that he
had been thinking that when Jesus Christ
made people 'to lie down in pleasant pastures,'
that it meant that he always fed them and
made them comfortable and happy first. There
were ever so many pretty little things said
about sheep and lambs, and some Bible verses
and bits of poetry recited, and some more
prayers and singing, and I really didn't think
we had been in the church ten minutes, when
the leader said the time had come to close.

"We all got back to the church again as
soon after breakfast as we could to the business meeting. I had made up my mind by
that time that those young folks could make
even business interesting, if they could do so
much with a half-hour prayer meeting. Besides,
I intended to find out all I could about this
queer society. The business was just as interesting as could be. They had a bright, quick
man for president, and he made things spin;
and they settled ever so many questions, and
made a dozen committees to attend to things
in less than no time, and then he called for
the reports from societies. It was just the most
amazing thing I ever did, to sit there and hear
all those young boys and girls and men and
women get up, one after another, and tell of
what their society was doing, how many mem-

bers it had, when it was formed, how it had grown and all sorts of things about it. They kept calling for new places all the time, and I just expected they would call for Parkerstown next, and I would have to get up and say we hadn't any society here, and never had even heard of it. I was so ashamed of Parkerstown that I didn't know what to do. But they didn't call for it. That afternoon there were two speeches about doing work for Christ, and there were papers five minutes long from different people, telling the best ways of working on the different committees they have in the society, Lookout and Social and Prayer meeting and all those things. I can't remember the rest of them, but I have a constitution at home in my trunk, and that will tell you what they all mean if you want to see it. They gave some nice ideas that made me wish we had a society here, so we could do some of the things they told about.

"It was great fun in the evening when the secretary came. He is the great secretary, you know, of the 'National', and they felt very proud to think he had promised to come to their convention, because he is so busy that he can't always go to all the conventions. He came in on the evening train, and came right down to the church without even a chance to wash his hands. We were singing when he came

in, because we had been kind of waiting along
for the train to come, and at the end of the
verses we all waved our handkerchiefs at him
as he came up to the platform. He was a
splendid-looking young man, real young; you
would hardly have thought him more than a
boy at first, though when you looked at him
closer you saw that he was a good deal older,
and he didn't talk like any boy, I can tell
you. He just stood up there and made everybody love him at first. He told us how glad he
was to see us, and how he had come a long
journey just to be with us. Then we were all
so glad he had come, and began to wonder
how we had gotten along with our convention
so far without him and called it a good time;
and we felt right away how sorry we should
be when the next day was over and we should
have to say goodby to him. He talked beauti-
fully. I wish I could tell you all the stories he
told us, and what wonderful things he said we
could do if each one did his part. I have some
of the things down in my little blank book,
and when I come over next time I'll bring it,
and then I can tell you more of his talk. He
didn't talk very long, and then we all went
home and went to sleep.

"The next morning's prayer meeting was
just as good as the first one, and a little better
because the secretary was there, and somehow

he made us feel as if Jesus Christ were a good deal nearer to us since he came, because he seemed to love him so very much. The next day there were reports and business and talks and a question-drawer where everybody asked questions on paper and the secretary answered them, and there was a story read, a beautiful story. I'll tell you that, all by itself, another time. It's too long for now. It was a Christian Endeavor story, too; everything was Christian Endeavor. Early in the evening there was a big reception in the town hall. Everybody went and shook hands with the secretary. I was introduced to him too, and he smiled just as cordially at me as he did to the people he stayed with and must have known a good deal better. Then about nine o'clock we all went to a procession to the church for the closing consecration meeting.

"Why, Harley, I never went to anything like that meeting! I can't begin to tell you anything about it. There were almost a hundred prayers in just about ten minutes. The singing was so sweet; everybody was much in earnest; and it seemed as if Jesus was right there in the room waiting to give a blessing to everyone, to me just as much as any one else. Everybody talked too, and told what the convention had done for them, and how it had helped them. I had to tell too, just a little word. I felt as if it would be ungrateful to go away from that meeting without saying how happy I felt for having been allowed to be there, and how I wanted so much to belong to that society, only we hadn't any to belong to, but I thought I would try by myself; and then some one came to me afterwards and told me he hoped I would begin a society, that I would likely find someone else to help, and that we would have a Christian Endeavor in our town before the next year's convention. Of course I didn't tell them what a hard place Parkerstown is, but I did wish with all my heart I had a society to come home to and join. I've been going to the one in Lewiston all the time I've been there, and they made me join; so I'm really a member after all.

"Well, the delegates mostly left by the midnight train, and we all went down to the station and had another reception and sort of praise-meeting there. The strangers seemed a little astonished at the queer set of young people who were singing and talking about religion. I heard one man say he never came across any like them before, but I guess it didn't do him any harm, for he threw away his cigar and went and had a long talk with the secretary. Aren't you tired now, Harley, and don't you want me to stop?"

No, Harley was not tired one bit, and he had a great many questions to ask. They were

answered patiently and carefully by one who
had such an intense interest in the subject
that it was a pleasure to her to explain even
the driest detail.

CHAPTER III

"If you can be a society all by yourself why couldn't I join?" asked Harley at last. "I should like to be a society. I couldn't do anything of course, but it would be nice to say I belonged to something like other boys. You said there were two kinds of members, didn't you? What are they? Tell me again. Why couldn't I be one of that other kind?"

"Yes; we have two kinds of members," answered Lois, unconsciously using the pronoun "we" in that connection for the first time, "active and associate, but the associate members are not much. They can't even vote. It is just to get hold of people and make them feel that they belong, you know. A real member ought to be an active member, I should think. You see the associate members are not Christians. An associate member is a kind of 'half-way' thing, any way. Why couldn't you be an active one?"

"Why, what would I have to do? I don't 'act' any. I just have to lie here and 'be'," said the boy, with a quiver about his mouth. "Oh, don't, Harley dear!" cried Lois, with tears in her eyes. "Yes, you could be an active member. You could give yourself to Jesus and sign the active membership pledge and keep it just as well as I can, and you would find lots of little bits of work to do for Christ right here in your own room."

Harley looked thoughtful and shook his head.

"I'm afraid I couldn't be much of a Christian," he said, "for you see, sometimes when my head aches so bad I'm cross. I have to be, and then it kind of gets the hurt out a little if I talk scolding to them, and make them give me my own way. But maybe I might. What did you say was the pledge again? I'd like to have it to think about a while. It would be nice to be a member of something. If I was 'active' we could have business meetings and I could vote, couldn't I? That would be lots of fun. But it wouldn't be right to think about that part of it unless I was really to sign my pledge and keep it, would it?"

"No," Lois admitted that she did not think it would. "I'll tell you what we can do, Harley," she said, "I can't remember the whole pledge but I'll write out the part that I said off to you and you can think that over, and when I go home I will write to the place in Boston where they keep the pledge-cards, and we'll each have a pledge-card to keep. It will be nice, I think, if we are going to be a society. You will like that, won't you?"

Harley showed his appreciation of it by

the brightness of his eyes.

So the first half of the pledge was written out and placed under Harley's pillow for further consideration. Lois said she must go home, and Harley followed her with wistful looks, then closed his eyes to think of all she had told him, and to sleep a little while with pleasant dreams of it.

It was three or four days before Lois found time to run up to see her little friend again. He had awaited her coming with great impatience, and now he drew the rumpled slip of paper from under his cushion and said as she entered the room:

"I think I can sign it, Lois. I've thought it all over and I'll try to keep it. You see, that first sentence helped me a good deal. It says, 'Trusting in the Lord Jesus Christ for strength.' I thought I couldn't be good all the time, but if I trust in Him to help me when I can't, why then I've nothing else to do but be as good as I can and then He'll do the rest. It isn't like promising some one else, either, that wouldn't understand when I was doing my best, and when the pain was so hard that I had to cry just a little. He'll always know when I'm doing my best, and it's Him I'll have to promise and not any one else. It doesn't seem hard to do what He wants me to do, for that isn't much now, but to lie still and be patient, and be willing to give up when I can't have what I want. I think I can promise that. And then of course, I can read the Bible a little while, and pray. I haven't always done it. Sometimes I would think it wasn't any use, and sometimes there was something I would want to do instead, like hearing a story or thinking about some plan I had made to amuse myself, and so I would forget to pray, but I guess I will join, Lois, if there isn't anything else in the pledge to promise."

Lois bent down and kissed the pure, white forehead and, looking into the eager, earnest eyes, felt that she would have a true little Christian for her co-laborer in the Christian Endeavor Society.

"The pledge-cards have come, Harley," she said, as she took her seat by his bed. "Didn't they come quickly? I ran right over with them because I thought you'd be in a hurry to see them. They came on the noon mail."

Harley reached an eager hand for the card and read it slowly, his face growing sober as he read.

"What kind of meetings does it mean I must be 'present at'?" he asked, "and what is a 'consecreation' meeting?"

Lois explained carefully about the prayer meetings and the monthly consecration meeting at which the roll was called and each member responded to his name by telling of his progress during the past month or by repeating a verse from the Bible.

"Could you and I have prayer meetings here in my room, do you mean, Lois? And, Lois, who would pray?"

Lois had thought of these questions a little and had made up her mind to do her duty and try to begin a Christian Endeavor Society right here, but it was nevertheless with beating heart that she answered:

"Yes, I think we might, Harley, and I suppose if there was no one else here, you and I would have to pray."

Harley considered this a moment. "Of course," said he, "you could pray. Maybe I'd get so I could too, a little, but I don't know how very well. Anyhow, I'd try if God wants me to do that."

"Then we'll be a society. Here's a constitution, and I've subscribed for the Golden Rule. That's the paper that's all about Christian Endeavor Societies, and you shall have it to read every week. I had it sent to you so you would get it as soon as it came. I thought it would interest you."

"Oh, thank you, Lois dear! How good you are to me! I shall not have any more stupid days now you've come home. The summer was so very long without you! How nice it will be to have a paper to read myself and all about our society!"

"And now when shall we have our first meeting?" asked Lois.

After much discussion it was decided to hold the meetings on Sunday afternoons at three o'clock.

"Because," said Harley, "this would be something like going to church, and I have wanted to go to church for so long. Besides, I have great trouble with Sundays. They are quite long and there hasn't been much I could do with them. Franklin reads to me a good deal, but he always takes a walk in the woods on Sundays, and I don't think he quite enjoys reading the things that mother thinks fit Sunday best; so, if you please, I'd like it on Sunday afternoon."

The paper arrived before the first Sunday meeting, and was eagerly devoured by its owner. He read to himself as long as they would allow him, and then every member of the family was pressed into service until he knew the matter of that week's issue pretty thoroughly. He had a very clear idea of what a Christian Endeavor prayer meeting should be, and he had gained much information about the various committees and their workings.

"We can't be, just us two, Lois," he announced when she came in Sunday afternoon. "I've been reading about it, and if we are to be a society at all, we'll have to go to work "I've been reading about it, and if we are to be a society at all, we'll have to go to work and get in some more. Besides, we need a president and secretary and ever so many committees. There's the prayer meeting committee and the lookout. I guess we don't need a social one yet, for we'll be social enough, just us two. But the lookout committee seems to be the beginning of everything. We'll have to have a business meeting. We don't want to have that on Sunday, and we'd better have one right off Monday, and fix these things. Now begin. You'll have to lead the meeting today because you know how, and you must tell me what to do all along. I've been reading up about these things. Did you know there is a subject already picked out for every week? I think we'd better take that, don't you? It will be nice to think we are having the same kind of a meeting they are having everywhere else, and we can pretend there are more folks here, and pick out things for them to say and read."

Lois began her first meeting with a trembling heart. It was hard for her to do such a thing even before this little boy. But she read a few verses and then knelt down by Harley's bed and prayed: "Dear Jesus, wilt thou bless this little society of two, and help us to know how to work for thee as the other larger societies are doing? For Jesus' sake. Amen." And Harley followed without being asked, with:

"Dear Jesus, I thank thee for sending me word about this society. Please help me to be a good member and keep my pledge, and show me how I can work. Amen."

It was not a very long meeting, but it was a good one. The great army of Christian Endeavorers over the land, if they had been permitted to look in upon the two with the open Bible between them, might perhaps not have felt much inspiration from the sight; but there nevertheless was, in that small meeting, the true Christian Endeavor spirit. They had claimed the promise that "where two or three of you shall gather in my name, I will be with them," and God's spirit was indeed there.

"I have thought of Sallie Elder," said Harley, when the solemn Christian Endeavor parting words, "The Lord watch between me and thee when we are absent one from another" had been repeated, and they had pronounced their first prayer meeting concluded. "Sallie Elder doesn't know what to do with Sunday. She told me so the other day when she was over here. I guess we could get her in. I could send a note to her all about it. I should like to write it, and Pepper could take it to her. Do you think, Lois, that it would be wicked to put Pepper on the lookout committee? If he does part of the work he ought to belong, oughtn't he? It wouldn't be wrong, would it, Lois?"

Now Pepper was a very homely little dog, who lay curled in a heap at Harley's feet during the meeting, fast asleep, and at the mention of his name he pricked up his ears, opened his bright little wistful eyes up at the two, and thumped his tail pleadingly as much as to say, "Do take me in; I'll be a very good dog."

It was finally decided that Pepper should be a sort of "ex-officio" member of the committee, and should be sent after Sallie Edler before the next meeting.

Sallie accepted the invitation with delight and became an associate member immediately. Lois was glad at the addition; but when, next Sunday, Harley announced that his brother Franklin had asked for admittance to the society, or at least to the meetings, her heart beat fast, and there was consternation in her face. Admit Franklin Winters to the meetings! How could they! He was not a Christian. Indeed, he was known to have said many things which led one to think he did not much believe in the Bible. Lois had always liked him very much, but she was afraid of him. He might make fun of their meetings. But even as she thought that, her heart told her he would not do such a thing as that. Perhaps he only wished to come there to please his little brother. But who would pray if Franklin came? Surely she could not.

She had never prayed aloud before in her life until she went to Lewiston, and there only once or twice. It had been a little trial to think of having Sallie added to their number, but she had decided to bear that for the sake of the good they might be able to do, but now to have this young man come — oh! it would be dreadful! It would be an impossibility to pray, and yet what could she say to Harley? Moreover, it appeared that Franklin was waiting in the other room for admittance. Lois must answer quickly.

"Why, Harley," she said, and her voice trembled as she looked down and fumbled with some papers between the leaves of her Bible, "I am afraid your brother wouldn't enjoy it. It's just us, you know, and" —

"O, yes, he would!" broke in Harley. "I told him all about it, and he said, all of his own accord, that he wished we would let him come, and his eyes looked real 'want to' when he said it, and he asked ever so many questions about it; so he knows just what it is. He said he thought if Sallie came that he might, and that he'd like to ever so much."

Before Lois had time to reply Franklin appeared at the door with Sallie, and his pleasant eyes were upon Lois's face while he asked:

"You are going to let me come, too, aren't you? Harley said he thought you would be glad to have an addition. I can't do much, to be sure, but I think I might manage to conduct myself as honorably as Pepper here," and he gave the dog a pat on the head, which was highly appreciated.

joy it. It's just as, you know, and,"—

"O, yes, he would!" broke in Harley, "I told him all about it, and he said, all of his

CHAPTER IV

Franklin sat down then, and there was nothing for Lois to do but submit, although she would gladly have fled the house and her new-fledged Christian Endeavor Society and never come back any more. Harley was to lead the meeting, so she had nothing to do but await developments, but she sat with her eyes down and her whole body in a quiver. Harley asked her almost immediately to pray for the opening of the meeting. She knelt down with not a thought in her mind and scarcely a desire in her heart except that she might be helped to get out of this trying situation, and the help came. "Thine ears shall hear a word behind thee, saying, 'This is the way, walk ye in it . . . Now therefore go, and I will be with thy mouth and teach thee what thou shalt say.' "

Surely these promises were fulfilled for her that day. She had not known what to say nor how to say anything indeed, but the young man who knelt across the room listening was amazed, and found himself wondering if it was really Lois Peters who was talking in that sweet voice, apparently to some One who stood close beside her, and in whom she seemed to have the utmost confidence. He seemed to feel that he was being prayed about too, although his name was not uttered, and

for the first time in his life he believed that
there was something in religion which he did
not understand, a power that reached into the
heart-life as nothing else could do. Harley felt
the influence of that prayer too, as he took
up the petition where Lois left off:

"Please, dear God, we thank thee that
we have some new members in our society.
Help them to get to be active members pretty soon. Let Pepper be a good member, if he
is only a dog. He can run around and do the
errands I could do if I were like other boys.
Amen."

The little dog curled up on the bed beside his young master, opened his eyes and
raised his head inquiringly at the mention of
his name, but seeing Harley's eyes closed, he
rested his cold nose confidingly against Harley's clasped hands and closed his own eyes
until the Amen, when he gave a soft whine
of satisfaction and settled down among the
pillows again. Franklin's eyes were wet with
tears when he raised his face from his hands,
and Lois's face was grave, but little Sallie Elder was immovable on the edge of her chair,
with wide-open eyes, throughout the entire
service, uncertain just what to call the strange
performance to which she had been invited.
It was not until Harley read slowly and carefully a story from the Bible that she began

to be interested, and by and by when the reading was over and the meeting thrown open for remarks, she was persuaded into repeating her one Bible verse: "Suffer little children to come unto me."

Franklin, too, had consented to read a verse if he were allowed to come, and not being very familiar with the Bible himself, Harley had selected it for him.

That was the beginning of the Parkerstown Christian Endeavor Society. It is not needful that you should know what was read or said at that meeting. There was nothing original or remarkable in it. You might think it very commonplace, but to those who were gathered there it seemed not so. They had caught the spirit of Christian Endeavor, and even Franklin felt that there was a power there, greater than any other which he knew. He promised to come again if they would let him, and even volunteered to become a temporary member of the lookout committee until some more worthy member should come in. He would that week agree to bring in at least two to the next meeting. Lois's heart began to swell with the thought of a real society right there in Parkerstown, albeit she had scarcely gotten over her panic at the rapid development of her small scheme. It was something to be thought about and prayed over,

this, actually planning to speak and pray before people like Franklin Winters, every week.
She was not sure she would be able to do it,
though she recognized that a power higher
than her own had helped her that afternoon;
but would He always help? Surely He had
promised, but — she must get away by herself
and think it over. Happy for Lois that she had
learned lately to think such things over upon
her knees. The Lord presides over decisions
made there, and so it was with a less fear-
ful heart that she came to the next meeting,
having herself prevailed upon three young
girls to come with her.

Harley had been made president. First,
because they thought it would please him,
but he proved such a good president, with so
many wise and original little plans for the
growth of the society, that they came to feel
after all that they could not have chosen more
wisely. For Harley read all he could get hold
of, and he knew all about the great Christian
Endeavor Society; he knew all its principles
and the wisest ways of working; he knew
more about it than all the rest of Parkerstown put together. Moreover, he had time to
think and plan and, best of all, to pray, and
to grow, in this thinking and planning and
praying, daily like Jesus Christ. They all saw
the change in his life, even patient as it had
been heretofore. There was a wondrous beau-

ty growing in that face that spoke of an inward peace, and a sweet wisdom that had touched the child-heart and caused it to open like a flower.

It came about very gradually, the addition to the society. First, Franklin brought two boys, farm hands from a neighbor's house, and then little Sallie coaxed her older sister, and then all grew interested and the meetings became larger until it was hard to find chairs enough in the square white house by the roadside, and until Harley's little bedroom off the sitting-room became too small to contain all the members.

"Father," said Harley one evening, when he had been lying quite still for a long time with his eyes closed, so that they all began to step softly and talk in low tones, thinking him asleep, "I wish you would take me into the big south room tomorrow. I haven't been in there in two years, I guess, and I want to see it. I have a plan. Perhaps you won't like it, and if you don't I will not coax; but, father, I should like to go in there and see it."

"You shall go, my son," said the father, who could not deny Harley anything in these days. "What is your plan, my boy?"

"Well, father, if you and mother don't like it, I won't make any fuss, but it's something I think would be very nice. Do you think mother cares very much about that south room? I know it's the parlor, and there's all the best things in there, but she doesn't use it much only on Christmas days, and not much then nowadays. It seems too bad to have it using itself up in the dark when it would be so nice for our society. I shouldn't think it would hurt things very much — just once a week — would it? Or couldn't I have it for my bedroom and you move the things in here and have this for the parlor? Do you think it is a very ridiculous plan, father? Because if you do, you and mother, why, I said I wouldn't coax, but I'd like to have you think it over very hard before you say," he said pleadingly.

And so, after much calculation and some changing of household plans, with a few tears mingled by father and mother, it is true — tears of love for their afflicted little boy — the plan was carried out, and the front parlor of the Winters' household became the headquarters of the Parkerstown Christian Endeavor Society. It is true that the room had not been much used as a parlor, and that it afforded ample accommodation for the meetings of the society.

"In fact," said father Winters, "we don't need it and they do, and what Harley wants will please us better than anything else, any way."

There was much bustle of preparation after the decision was made. Franklin agreed to give as his part enough cane-seat chairs to accommodate the members. Some one sent a fine engraving of Father Endeavor Clark, Lois brought over a large copy of the United States Pledge, neatly framed, to hang over Harley's couch, and together she and Harley planned little decorations to make the room look home-like and yet "churchified," as Harley said. A great monogram C.E. was made from evergreen and hung in the center of one wall, surrounded by the motto, "For Christ and the Church." Another wall contained the motto, "One is your Master, even Christ, and all ye are brethren." Harley made Lois describe the mottoes she had seen at the convention in Lewiston, and they made theirs as much like them as possible. When the motto, "For Christ and the Church," was put up, Harley lay thinking long about it. He didn't see how he could be working for the Church at all. But the end of his thoughts was that he wanted the new minister asked to attend the meetings. The minister was invited, and came with a glad heart. He had heard of this society with thankfulness, but had not thought it best to come until invited. Now he became one with the young people, and helped them along more than they knew. He grew to love the little president much as did every one else, and came frequently to see him, finding that in this young disciple there was much of the spirit of Jesus, and that he might sit at his feet and gather inspiration and new love and faith from conversation with this sweet, trusting child.

The work of the society was carried on according to the most approved methods. No suggestion passed by unheeded. Everything, too, was talked over carefully with the minister, to see whether in their particular society such and such measures were expedient. Every member had a pledge-card. There were cards from the National Headquarters for the different committees to use in their work, and topic cards and everything else that could be thought of; for when Harley expressed a wish for a simple little thing like that to work with, there were plenty to see that it was granted; and so it came about that there was not in all the State, a society better fitted out for work in all departments, than the one at Parkerstown.

Harley had one thing of which he was very proud. The minister brought it to him one day when he came to see him. It was a Christian Endeavor scarf-pin of solid gold; and how Harley loved that pin! He looked at it for hours at a time thinking what it meant; he held it in the rays of sunlight that lay across his bed; he wore it pinned on the breast of his dressing-gown with pleasure, and showed it to every one that came to see him.

"It seems to shine brighter than any other gold thing," he said one day. "I wonder what makes it. Is it because it is for Christ?"

The meetings were large in those days, and very solemn ones. A good many of the Parkerstown young people were beginning to find out what it is to belong to Jesus Christ, and many others were seeking Him. Even the new big room was full every Sunday afternoon, and the songs that filled the air and floated out to the street often drew in outsiders who were taking a little walk or who had nothing else to do. Lois had sacrificed her organ to the cause, though it was not a sacrifice, but given gladly, and Franklin had brought it over himself, so they had good rousing singing and plenty of it, and Harley would lie on his little couch by the desk and look at the organ with admiring eyes, feeling that it lent a dignity of the church to the modest room.

But there were days, and growing more frequent now, when the little couch by the light desk was empty, and the young president of this society was unable to be moved in to the meeting, but must lie in the darkened bedroom beyond, with the door closed, and suffer. At first they thought the meetings must be adjourned when Harley was not able to be there, because the noise would trouble him, and because they felt they could not do without him, until he begged so hard that all should go on as usual that it was tried as an experiment, in hushed voices and without music. But Harley missed that at once and sent word for them to sing:

"At the cross, at the cross, where I
first saw the light,
And the burden of my heart rolled
away,
It was there by faith I received my sight,
And now I am happy all the day."

He said the singing rested him. So, after that they went on as usual, only when the president was not there, there was a more earnest feeling manifest in all the members, and much praying done that the dear boy might be relieved from his sufferings. Some who had not cared much about the meetings heretofore seemed strangely touched by the thought that the little, patient sufferer was lying there thinking of them and praying for them.

CHAPTER V

It was the evening of the day after one of these sad, painful Sabbaths. Lois and his brother Franklin were sitting by Harley's bed. They had been telling him about the meeting as he had asked them. Franklin let Lois do much of the talking, he only helping her out here and there when she forgot what came next, or called upon him to know who was present. He was not yet an active member, and apparently no nearer being a Christian than when the society was first organized. He came in regularly to the meetings and did whatever he was asked to do, even to reading a verse of Harley's selection, but he never selected one himself, and always kept in the background as much as possible. People said he was doing it all for his little brother's sake, and no one dared approach him upon the subject or even urge him to do more. Very few remembered to pray for him, I think, there were so many others worse than he, they thought. But Lois was praying, and so was his brother. Many a night when he could not sleep he lay and talked with God and asked him to make Franklin love Him.

"I want to tell you something," said Harley suddenly rousing from deep silence into which they had fallen. "I have seen something, and I think you would like to know about it. I should like it if you should see such a thing to have you tell me about it. It was last Sunday when you were at meeting. The pain in my eyes was so bad that I had to close them and my head ached very badly, so that I couldn't even have the bedroom door open to hear your voices in the room, but had to close my ears, too, to bear the pain. I could just hear the sound of the song you were singing. I do not remember what it was, but it was very sweet, though it seemed far away, and it grew further away, and further, until it suddenly seemed to turn and come back again and burst into the sweetest, clearest music you ever heard. It was like, and yet it was not like, the music in our meetings. It was such as that would be if every voice was perfect, perhaps the sort of singing they have in Heaven, though I never knew before that any singing could be sweeter than what we have in our meetings; but of course Heaven has everything better.

"Well, this singing, although it was very near and loud, didn't make my head ache a bit harder, and even seemed to rest my back; at least I forgot it was aching. There was a light all around, too, and I could look up without its hurting my eyes. I didn't think how strange that was then, but just listened to the music and looked at the light. It took a shape in some clouds that were far off and yet all around — you see you were not there and so I can't quite explain it all, because there wasn't time for me to understand everything about, and there was so much else to see. The light grew brighter and brighter and broadened out at the top as though a hundred suns were shining through one spot, and there was a long, sharp, golden crack in the clouds below, and the light changed and broadened and shaped and brightened in such a strange way until suddenly I thought of the shape of my Christian Endeavor pin, and then all at once I saw the letters at the top C.E., and the long sharp ray of light was the pin, and there it was in the clouds all gold, and growing 'golder' every minute, until I thought I couldn't look any longer; but I had to, because it was so beautiful. And then I saw that the line that made the pin was only a break in the clouds, where the light from Heaven — it must have been Heaven — shone through. Above, in the large, bright letters was a real opening into such light as you never saw before, and even when the sun sets; and then there came angels, hurrying out of the letters and down through the narrow opening and everywhere towards me, and more were beyond up there in the brightness. I watched them come out through the opening, and more and more of them seemed to come from the golden letters until all the air was full of them, and one angel came quite close to me and touched me on the shoulder where I lay —

right here in my room, just think — and he said: 'Little president' — he called me 'little president' just as the secretary did when he wrote to me that nice letter after I wrote him about our new society and told him how young I was — 'Dear little president,' he said, 'you are one of us now, for we are Christian Endeavorers too, though our work is different from yours, but it is going on all the time. We are the "ministering spirits." God our father loves your society and will bless it.' And then I felt it all so wonderful! I was just here in my bed, you know, and my head was aching so hard just a minute before, and there was the great piece of sky that I see from the window every day, and the hills at the foot of it, and there in the center of it the beautiful great gold badge, with the air full of lights and angels from it, and the most beautiful music floating all about. I was so glad and so astonished at it all that God should have taken so much trouble to send word to me, that I almost let the angel go away without saying anything but 'Thank you' to him; but just as he turned with a lovely smile to fly back, I asked him if he would please see that something was done for a few people down here in our society who didn't love Jesus. Then he put his hand on my head and smiled again, and there was a look in his eyes that I'm sure meant yes, so he went back into the center of the light again. I could see him all the way, just as clearly as when he stood beside me, and when he reached the very center of the brightness the music got farther away again, and the angels all went back, and the Heaven's badge grew dim, and pretty soon was all covered up, and I only heard the music; and pretty soon the music was the hymn you were singing in the other room, 'God be with you till we meet again,' and your meeting was breaking up. But I wish you could have seen it, and don't you think it was wonderful?"

Later, after Franklin had taken Lois home, and come back to kiss the little brother good-night, Harley put his arm about his neck and drew his face close down to his own.

"Frank," he whispered, with his lips to the young man's ear, "you were one of those that I asked the angel about, and I wanted him to be very sure about you, because I love you so much."

The older brother finished the good-night greeting hastily, and drew away to hide his emotion, but there was a warmth in the quick grasp that he gave the little hand, that Harley knew meant that he understood and appreciated.

Now about this time there fell to the

lot of that society a bit of good fortune and happiness such as they had not dreamed of. The society which had been expected to entertain the State convention in the spring was somewhat disabled, and wrote to say that they must withdraw their invitation, whereupon the State secretary and executive committee, having heard of the rapid growth of the Parkerstown Society wrote to know if they would like to entertain the convention. Ah! Wouldn't they? Such honor was almost enough to take the breath away! The dear young president was so excited that they almost had to keep him away from the next Sunday's meeting. To have a real convention right there in their society, the first year, and the national secretary coming to it, too, and perhaps — oh, wonderful hope! — perhaps, the dear Father Endeavor himself — for that was the hope that the State secretary held out to them.

"O, Lois!" he said, with his eyes shining very brightly, and his hands clasped tightly together with excitement, "this must have been part of what the angel meant when he came out of the letters in the sky and said God would bless our society. I can't go to much of the convention myself, of course, because our room will not be large enough, and the meetings will have to be held in the church, but you can tell me all about them as you do Sundays about the service, and we shall have some real delegates in the house to talk to, for mother said so; she said we could have four. Just think, and that perhaps they would be willing if the secretary and Father Endeavor came, that they would stop here on account of my not being able to go out to hear them. Do you think others would mind and think me very greedy? Because I should want to have a little of them you know, and then perhaps they would have just one meeting here in our room. The consecration meeting would be so grand, or a morning prayer meeting; I should so like it!"

It was decided that the convention should come, and there was much looking forward to it, and the meetings grew in interest and spirituality.

"Oh," said Harley one afternoon at the close of the meeting, "I wish that every day was Sunday! If only our meetings could last longer. I did not want it to be out today at all."

But the mother looked anxiously at her boy, and was thankful in her heart that every day was not filled with excitement for him. It was getting more and more apparent to the ones who were watching him closely, that Harley was not to stay with them much longer. They had questioned whether the meetings which were so dear to him were not, after all, doing him harm, and perhaps ought to be stopped; but the wise doctor shook his head sadly, and said:

"No; if he is careful not to get too excited, it can do but little harm. The disease will have its way, do what we will. The end is not far off, I fear, but I do not think that will hasten it. The boy is getting to be such a power in this community that I do not see how we can do without him." And he went slowly from the room with bent head, while the mother covered her face with her hands, and sat down to silent grief.

Spring was coming. The convention time was near at hand, when the summons came to the little president to leave his society. He had been very ill for a whole week. On Sunday the society had met in the south room but to pray through the whole hour. Lois and Franklin were near Harley constantly. He could not bear to have them out of his sight.

It was the balmiest morning the spring had given them yet. The birds were trying some summer carols, and the breeze brought a few stray notes in at the open window. But to those in the room the notes had a sad sound, that told of some great change about to come. The whole family were gathered about Harley's bed, for he had passed through a night of suffering, and Dr. Fremont had told them he could not last much longer. He suddenly opened his eyes and looked up as Lois softly entered the room, her arms full of the splendid white lilies he loved so much.

"Lois," he said, smiling, and putting out his thin little hand to touch the flowers, "I don't think I can stay to the convention here after all. I'm sorry not to see the secretary and Father Endeavor and all the delegates, but I think I can't stay. I saw the badge in the sky again this morning; it was brighter than before, and the angel came and spoke to me, and he said there was a convention in Heaven now, and they wanted me for a delegate from Parkerstown, and I'm to stay, Lois. The delegates to that convention all stay, and it's to get ready for the great convention when you're all coming — the angel told me so. And I don't feel so bad about not seeing Father Endeavor and the secretary now, for they will come to the great convention pretty soon. It's only a little while, and I'm to see Jesus, you know. Besides, I shall be able to do real work up there, and not have to lie on a bed, as I do here. He promised me. He asked me whom I would have to do my work for me if I went, and I told him I didn't think it mattered about that, that I was only a little invalid boy down here, and that I had been doing pieces of other people's work. But he said no; I had a work of my own, and that I must give it to some one else to do. I thought of you, Lois, but I decided that you had enough of your own work to do, so I told him that I thought my brother Franklin would do it. You will, won't you, Franklin? You'll have to give yourself to Jesus, you know, and then you can do it, and you didn't have a work of your own. So he said it would be all right. You will, won't you, Franklin?"

The strong young man bowed his head on the pillow beside his brother and grasped the dear little hand held out so pleadingly, promising to take the commission. Harley's other worn white hand went feebly up to his breast, where was fastened the beloved gold pin, which he wore night and day. He took it off, and tried to fasten it in Franklin's coat, but was too weak to do so.

"Put it on and keep it. The angel told me I wouldn't need it up there, because he would introduce me as the delegate from Parkerstown, and they would know all about me. I think I know what makes that pin shine so now; it's the light from the letters in Heaven, that catches all the pins in the earth. You'll take good care of it, Franklin, won't you? and you'll take my place and work with Lois. She-'ll show you how. I wish you would find a verse to read for me at the next consecration meeting. I'm sorry not to be there, and oh! if you would say something for me at the consecration meeting of the convention I should like it, because I can't be there, you know; and if they should call my name I should like some answer to be made to it. Good-by, mother and father, I must go now, the light is coming in the sky again, and the angel will be here for me. I thought I caught a glimpse of the throne when the letters opened the last time and maybe I shall see Jesus right away. Good-by."

And the little president of one winter passed into the "Great Convention which never breaks up," and to the "Sabbath which has no end," having accomplished more for Christ during his short winter than many of us do in a lifetime.

"Weep if we may — bend low as ye pray!
What does it mean?
Listen! God fashioned a house. He said:
      'Build it with care'.
Then softly laid the soul
      To dwell in there.

"And always he watched it — guarded it so,
      Both day and night;
The wee soul grew as your lilies do,
      Splendid and white.

"It grew, I say, as your lilies grow,
    Tender and tall;
Till God smiled, 'Now the house is too low
    For the child, and small.'

"And gently he shut the shutters one night,
    And closed the door;
'More room and more light to walk upright
    On a Father's floor.' "

The End of the Parkerstown Delegate